STEM IN THE SUPER BOWL

BY MIKE DOWNS

CONTENT CONSULTANT

JESSE WILCOX, PHD
ASSISTANT PROFESSOR OF STEM EDUCATION
SIMPSON COLLEGE

SportsZone
An Imprint of Abdo Publishing
abdobooks.com

WOODRIDGE PUBLIC LIBRARY
Three Plaza Drive
Woodridge, IL 60517-5017

ABDOBOOKS.COM

Published by Abdo Publishing, a division of ABDO, PO Box 398166, Minneapolis, Minnesota 55439. Copyright © 2020 by Abdo Consulting Group, Inc. International copyrights reserved in all countries. No part of this book may be reproduced in any form without written permission from the publisher. SportsZone™ is a trademark and logo of Abdo Publishing.

Printed in the United States of America, North Mankato, Minnesota
092019
012020

THIS BOOK CONTAINS RECYCLED MATERIALS

Cover Photo: Lionel Hahn/Abaca/Sipa USA/AP Images
Interior Photos: Al Messerschmidt/AP Images, 4–5; Kevin Terrell/AP Images, 7, 38–39; Ross D. Franklin/AP Images, 9; Rick Scuteri/AP Images, 10; Paul Spinelli/AP Images, 12–13, 27; Michael Conroy/AP Images, 14; Red Line Editorial, 16, 40; Dave Eulitt/Kansas City Star/MCT/Tribune News Service/Getty Images, 19; Heinz Kluetmeier/Sports Illustrated/Getty Images, 20–21, 35; James Lee/iStockphoto, 22 (stadium); Shutterstock Images, 22 (camera); George Gojkovich/Getty Images Sport/Getty Images, 28–29; Adam Bettcher/Getty Images Sport/Getty Images, 31; Akili-Casundria Ramsess/Atlanta Journal-Constitution/AP Images, 33; Al Pereira/Getty Images Sport/Getty Images, 36; Win McNamee/Getty Images Sport/Getty Images, 45

Editor: Marie Pearson
Series Designer: Dan Peluso

LIBRARY OF CONGRESS CONTROL NUMBER: 2019941988

PUBLISHER'S CATALOGING-IN-PUBLICATION DATA
Names: Downs, Mike, author.
Title: STEM in the Super Bowl / by Mike Downs
Description: Minneapolis, Minnesota : Abdo Publishing, 2020 | Series: STEM in the greatest sports events | Includes online resources and index.
Identifiers: ISBN 9781532190575 (lib. bdg.) | ISBN 9781644943151 (pbk.) | ISBN 9781532176425 (ebook)
Subjects: LCSH: Super Bowl--Juvenile literature. | Sports sciences--Juvenile literature. | Applied science--Juvenile literature. | American football--Juvenile literature. | Physics--Juvenile literature.
Classification: DDC 796.015--dc23

TABLE OF CONTENTS

1 SUPER STEM 4

2 THE SCIENCE OF WINNING 12

3 ADVANCING WITH TECHNOLOGY . 20

4 ENGINEERING STADIUMS AND EQUIPMENT 28

5 MATH IN ACTION 38

GLOSSARY 46
MORE INFORMATION 47
ONLINE RESOURCES 47
INDEX 48
ABOUT THE AUTHOR 48

Steve McNair throws a pass in Super Bowl XXXIV.

CHAPTER 1

SUPER STEM

The crowd roars inside the Georgia Dome. It is the final play of Super Bowl XXXIV on January 30, 2000. Indoors it's 72 degrees Fahrenheit (22°C). Outside, a frigid ice storm has raged for three days. The score is St. Louis Rams 23, Tennessee Titans 16. The Titans have the ball at the Rams' 10-yard line with six seconds remaining. That's time enough for a single play. A touchdown by the Titans would provide a new statistic for Super Bowls. It would be the first ever to go into overtime.

Five yards behind the line of scrimmage, Steve McNair, the Titans' quarterback, takes the snap. He judges the different speeds and angles of the rapidly moving players. If a defender charges toward him too quickly, he needs to dart away or throw the ball early. Hearing the crunch of pads nearby, he knows he's being protected. He prepares to throw the ball. McNair searches downfield as his receivers run their preplanned routes. He won't throw the ball at the receiver. Instead, he will fire the ball to a point well in front of his receiver. Years of practice have taught him the geometry of the game. The angle and speed of both the ball and the receiver are carefully planned to meet at a specific point. He spots Kevin Dyson sprinting on a slant route. He is open at the 5-yard line. McNair fires the ball. It's caught! The crowd howls, some with joy, others with disappointment. But the play is not over yet.

As Dyson races the short distance to the goal line, another force comes into play. That force is Mike Jones. The Rams' linebacker leaps for Dyson. He grabs him by

Mike Jones's tackle saved the game for the Rams.

the legs and hangs on. It's only two yards to the goal line. Dyson makes a last frantic leap toward the end zone. He stretches out. Two yards. One yard. And then it's over. Jones's heavier body and glue-like grip have kept Dyson from scoring the touchdown. The goal line remains inches away from Dyson's outstretched arm. The Rams win Super Bowl XXXIV.

TOUCHDOWNS WITH STEM

Every Super Bowl game provides lessons in the fields of science, technology, engineering, and math (STEM). Many aspects of science, including wind direction, weather, and the size and speed of players affect every Super Bowl differently. From field condition to coaching techniques, science is always a part of the game.

Technology is also a factor. Buying tickets, entering the stadium, selling concessions, providing security, and broadcasting the game all depend on advanced technology. Security uses facial-recognition scanners, metal detectors, and radiation- and bomb-detection devices. Cameras provide many views of the action.

The engineering marvels of indoor stadiums have also changed the game. In the past, Super Bowls weren't held in northern states because of cold temperatures. A 2016 playoff game between the Minnesota Vikings and Seattle Seahawks was played outdoors at the University of Minnesota in Minneapolis. The Vikings' new

Super Bowl security requires a lot of technology because of the large number of fans who come to watch.

stadium was under construction. During this game, the teams endured temperatures down to minus-6 degrees Fahrenheit (minus-21°C). Compare this to Super Bowl LII, only two years later, on February 4, 2018. It was also played in Minneapolis, where the temperature at kickoff was 3 degrees Fahrenheit (minus-16°C). But instead of

Different types of cleats work better on different types of playing surfaces.

freezing, the New England Patriots and Philadelphia Eagles played indoors in a comfortable 70 degrees Fahrenheit (21°C) at the new U.S. Bank Stadium.

Stadiums aren't the only things in sports that need engineering. Players' equipment is also highly engineered. Shoes have cleats made of cutting-edge materials, specially designed for each position and type of turf. Sticky gloves help players catch balls.

Math is used in every part of the game. At what angle and speed should the quarterback throw the ball? How fast should a wide receiver run? Math explains why each play works or does not work. Or consider the never-ending statistics. Which Super Bowl–winning team had the worst regular-season record? It was the 2011 New York Giants, with a 9–7 record. Which teams have won the most Super Bowls? The Patriots and Pittsburgh Steelers each won six of the first 53 Super Bowls.

Multiple coaches working together can develop better approaches to each game than a single coach could.

CHAPTER 2

THE SCIENCE OF WINNING

The science of winning a football game starts with the head coach. He has responsibility to make decisions that will lead his team to the Super Bowl. He is supported by a staff of assistant coaches who have more specialized duties. Working together, the coaching staff decides which players make the team and which positions they will play. The coaches develop plays that use each of their athletes to the best advantage. They watch hours of video analyzing other teams. Then they decide how to best compete against them. All of

Players had to fight pouring rain in Super Bowl XLI.

this is done through a combination of data collection, scientific analysis, and the head coach's judgment. Every decision affects the outcome of each game.

WEATHERING THE GAME

There are some things that a head coach cannot control, such as the weather. Super Bowl XLI proved that to be true. In 2007, the city of Miami, Florida, hosted the Indianapolis Colts and Chicago Bears in the wettest Super Bowl on record. Nearly 1 inch (2.5 cm) of rain fell during the game. Bears quarterback Rex Grossman fumbled twice. He said the ball would just slip out of his hands. The trouble playing with a slippery ball lasted the entire game. In the first quarter, there were two consecutive fumbles. With less than seven minutes

MARTIAL ARTS ON THE FIELD

Size isn't everything. Training in martial arts can teach smaller players how to take advantage of a larger opponent. Lawrence Taylor, a Hall of Fame pass rusher in the 1980s, was one of the first to use martial arts training to improve his skills in football. Many teams now use martial arts techniques in their training. Physics can explain why these techniques work.

STICKY BUMPS

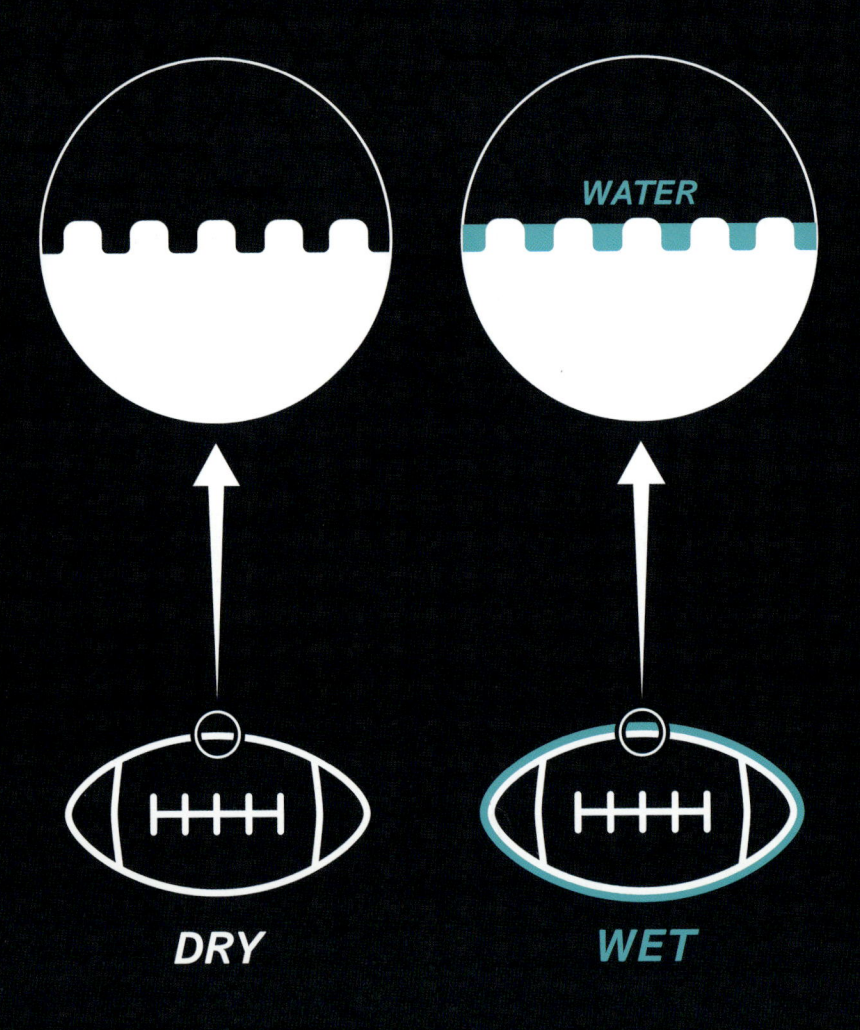

WATER

DRY **WET**

The skin of a football is covered with tiny bumps. The bumps help players grip the ball. A player's hand squishes into the bumps, creating friction, when the football is dry. However, when water contacts the football, it fills the empty spaces, making the football more difficult to grip. Less grip on the football means less friction, and most likely more fumbles.

remaining in the first quarter, the Colts punted to the Bears. Gabe Reid caught the ball and returned it to the Bears' 35-yard line. He was hit and fumbled the ball. The Colts recovered.

On the very next play, Colts quarterback Peyton Manning fumbled the ball as he attempted a handoff. The Bears recovered the ball with a slippery, sliding grab. These were only two of the six fumbles from that game. What contributed to the fumbles? The rain. Or more precisely, the lack of friction. Water on a football makes it slippery and hard to control.

SPECIALIZED POSITIONS

Player positions have become more specialized. In the early days of football, players had to play many positions, both offensive and defensive. Today, teams have larger rosters. In Super Bowl LIII on February 3, 2019, each team had 46 active players. Each player is now specially trained for a certain position. For instance, the wide receiver position requires quickness and the ability to run long distances. These players add only the muscle they need to achieve higher speeds. Any more body weight would need more energy to accelerate and run. In positions needing bulk, more weight can help. Linemen weigh more than receivers because they must power their way through opponents. The added weight can increase their momentum and hitting power. Momentum is a combination of the amount of matter in a person or object and speed in a certain direction.

Over time specialized training has changed the body types of certain positions. On January 15, 1967, the Green Bay Packers played the Kansas City Chiefs in Super Bowl I. On offense, the average weight of the centers was 240 pounds (109 kg). In Super Bowl LIII, the average weight of the centers was 306 pounds (139 kg). The same holds true when comparing defensive tackles. In Super Bowl I the average defensive tackle weighed 264 pounds (120 kg). By Super Bowl LIII, the average weight of a defensive tackle was 316 pounds (143 kg). That's an astonishing 28 percent increase in average

Different body types are ideal for different positions.

weight for centers and 20 percent increase for tackles. However, the opposite occurred for wide receivers. These players need speed. In Super Bowl I, wide receivers averaged 215 pounds (98 kg). In Super Bowl LIII, their average weight was only 196 pounds (89 kg), approximately 9 percent less.

Skycam is one of the most noticeable cameras at the Super Bowl.

CHAPTER 3

ADVANCING WITH TECHNOLOGY

Every year, millions of fans around the world get together to celebrate and cheer for their favorite teams. Even from thousands of miles away, fans can follow the game. They can watch it as if they were standing on the sidelines or hovering above the field. This is possible with lots of cameras.

EYES EVERYWHERE

Overhead, Skycam provides the bird's eye view. It hangs on four wires, hovering above the action. A pilot controls the reels of

EYE IN THE SKY

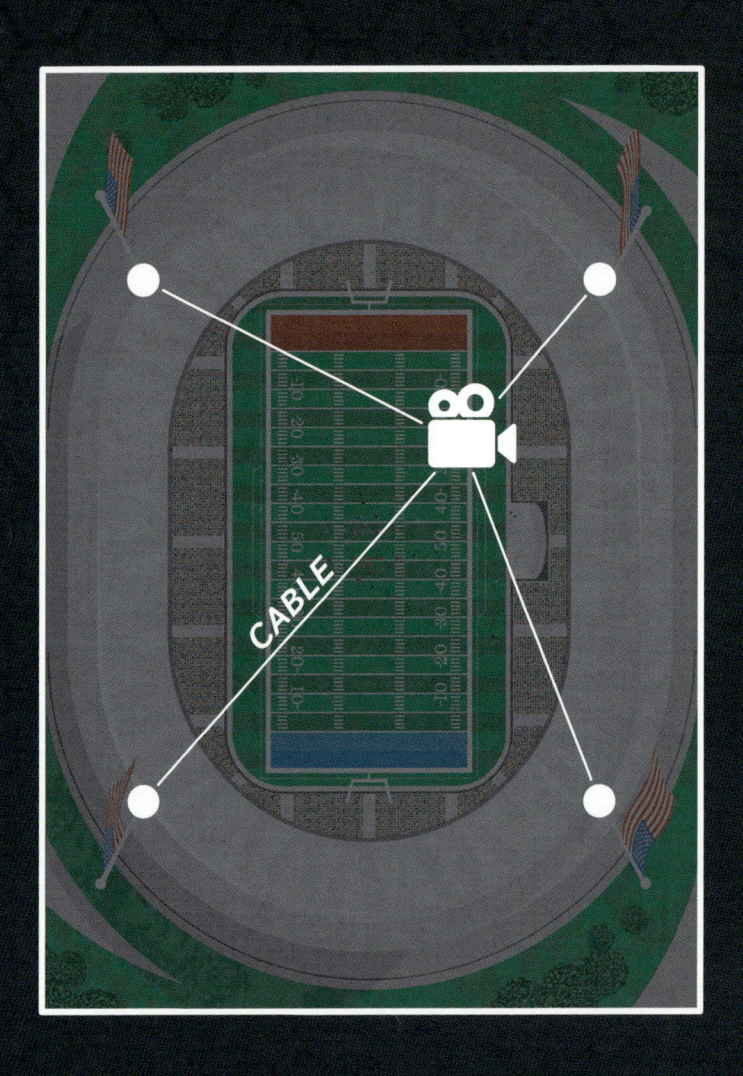

CABLE

Skycam hangs over the field ready to capture the action. It's connected to four computer-controlled reels, one at each corner of the stadium. Each reel has 1,400 feet (425 m) of cable that is quickly reeled in or out based on the Skycam pilot's commands. A fiber optic cable sends video images from the camera to the control booth.

wire, whizzing the camera around. A separate operator controls the camera itself. Other cameras spaced around the field project computerized images onto television screens. These include the first down line and the line of scrimmage.

End zone pylons house more cameras. When a touchdown is too close to call, these cameras can make the difference. In Super Bowl LI on February 5, 2017, referees relied on the cameras. After the biggest comeback in Super Bowl history, the Patriots tried to win the game with a touchdown in overtime. Running back James White powered his way through the defense, stretching for the end zone. Three Atlanta Falcons defenders wrestled him to the ground. The football barely reached the goal line. Was it good? Or did White's knee hit the ground first? The pylon cameras had the answer. The touchdown was good. The Patriots had won another Super Bowl.

INSTANT REPLAY

On-field officials normally make the correct call, but sometimes coaches don't agree. Today's technology allows a quick solution. Using the many cameras available, replay officials gather the best shots of the play to make a decision.

In the early days of football, cameras were found only on the sidelines. Close calls were never reviewed on film. The referee's call was final. The NFL first tried instant replay in the 1970s. But at the time, broadcasters did not use enough cameras to get clear angles on each play.

HALFTIME TECH

Technology affects more than the game. Halftime shows have radically changed from their simple beginnings. In Super Bowl XI, played on January 9, 1977, the audience participated by holding up colored cards. Today, technology highlights the entertainment. In Super Bowl XLVII, played on February 3, 2013, singer Beyoncé took center stage. She danced on a stage of multi-colored video graphics synchronized to her music. The stage consisted of 20 interconnected platforms with computer-coordinated graphics.

Officials estimated they needed at least 12 cameras in the stadium to catch all angles.

Instant replay returned in the 1986 season. On January 25, 1987, Super Bowl XXI between the Denver Broncos and New York Giants used instant replay. Television network CBS handled the broadcast. Late in the first half, the Broncos led 10–7 and had the ball close to their own end zone. A pass to Broncos tight end Clarence Kay was ruled incomplete. Officials used instant replay to check the ruling. The one angle CBS provided was unclear. The ruling stood. Later, CBS finally found an angle that showed it should have been ruled a catch. But it was too late to change the call. The next play, the Giants got a safety when they sacked Denver quarterback John Elway in the end zone. The Giants went on to win the game. If CBS hadn't been slow to find the right angle, the safety would never have happened.

Today's technology has changed that completely. Now fans can see every play from a variety of angles.

Replays are nearly instantaneous. A lack of camera angles is no longer an issue. In Super Bowl XLIX, on February 1, 2015, NBC had 40 cameras working to capture the action. By Super Bowl LIII, CBS had stationed 115 cameras around the stadium. These included the overhead Skycam, 14 used for producing virtual graphics, 28 pylon cameras in the end zones and 72 other cameras. Improvements to technology mean that by the time the referee is ready, all good angles of the play are ready for review on a tablet. Of all calls reviewed, approximately four out of 10 are reversed.

Despite all of these advancements in technology, instant replay is set into motion by one very simple technology. A coach throws a red challenge flag onto the field. Sometimes, a simple tool works best!

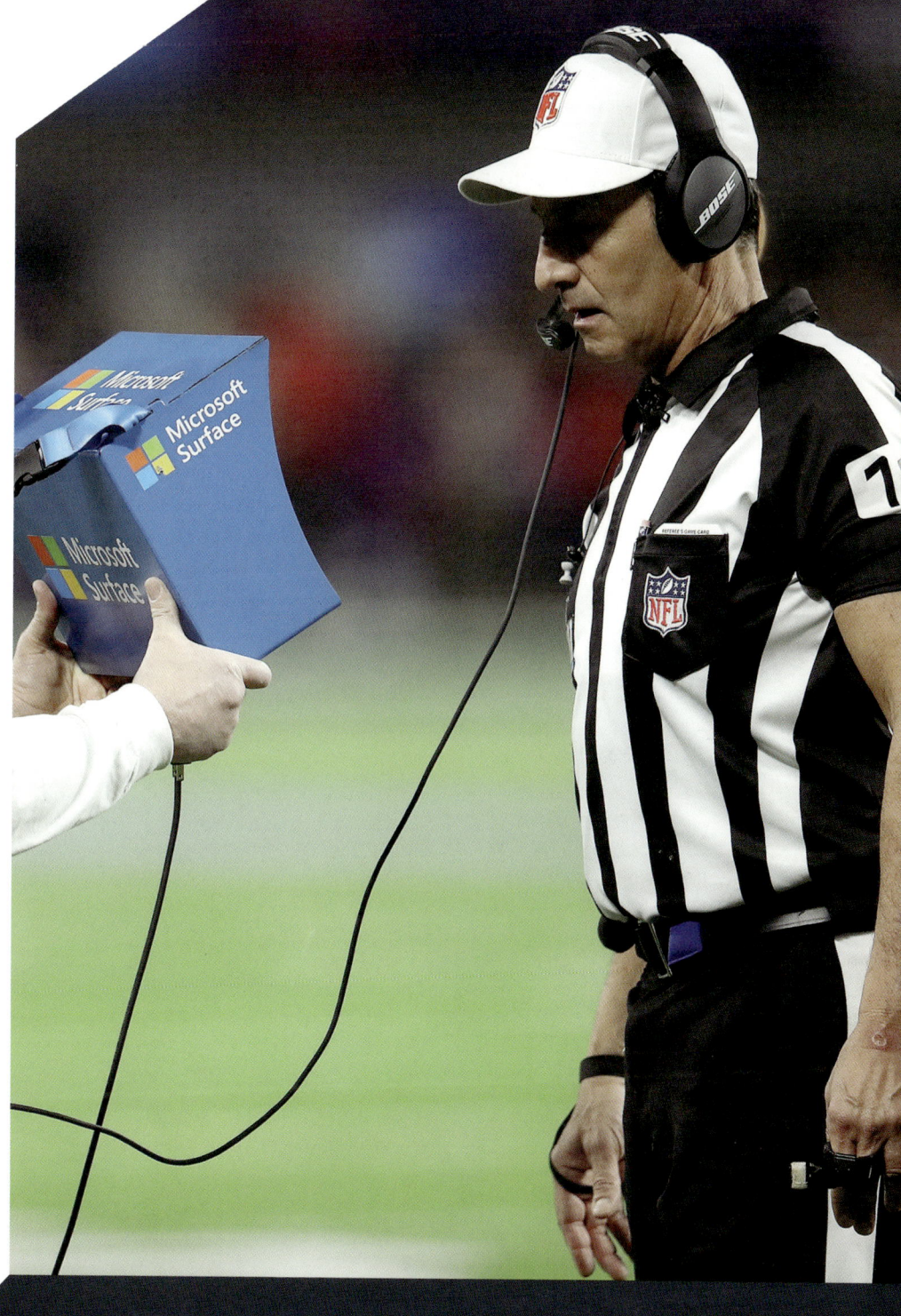

Referees can watch replays on the sidelines thanks to tablets.

Although it was cold and icy in Detroit, Michigan, the indoor stadium kept fans and players warm during Super Bowl XVI.

28

CHAPTER 4

ENGINEERING STADIUMS AND EQUIPMENT

Most Super Bowls take place in warm-weather cities. Super Bowl games are played in midwinter. However, with the introduction of indoor stadiums, northern states could finally host Super Bowls.

Of 53 Super Bowls, only six have been played in the north. Super Bowl XVI on January 24, 1982, was the first in a northern state. It took place in Detroit, Michigan, at the Pontiac Silverdome. Like many indoor stadiums, the Silverdome was a marvel of engineering. It was famous for its air-supported roof made of plastic and fiberglass.

Minneapolis hosted Super Bowl LII. As winter froze the city, players and fans enjoyed the comfort of being indoors. They also enjoyed the glass structure and see-through roof. The roof, made of a strong, plastic-like material, allows natural light to filter through while still providing protection from the weather. Engineers harnessed the clear roof's ability to capture heat from the sun. Heat collects near the roof. That warm air gets pumped down through the stands and onto the field.

Some southern states also have indoor stadiums. For them, rain or heat is more of a problem than snow. Super Bowl LIII was played at Mercedes-Benz Stadium in Atlanta, Georgia. Its retractable roof has eight triangular pieces. Each piece weighs 500 tons (450 metric tons). When activated, it looks like the petals of a flower twisting open. But each petal is actually moved straight

HEAT RESERVOIR

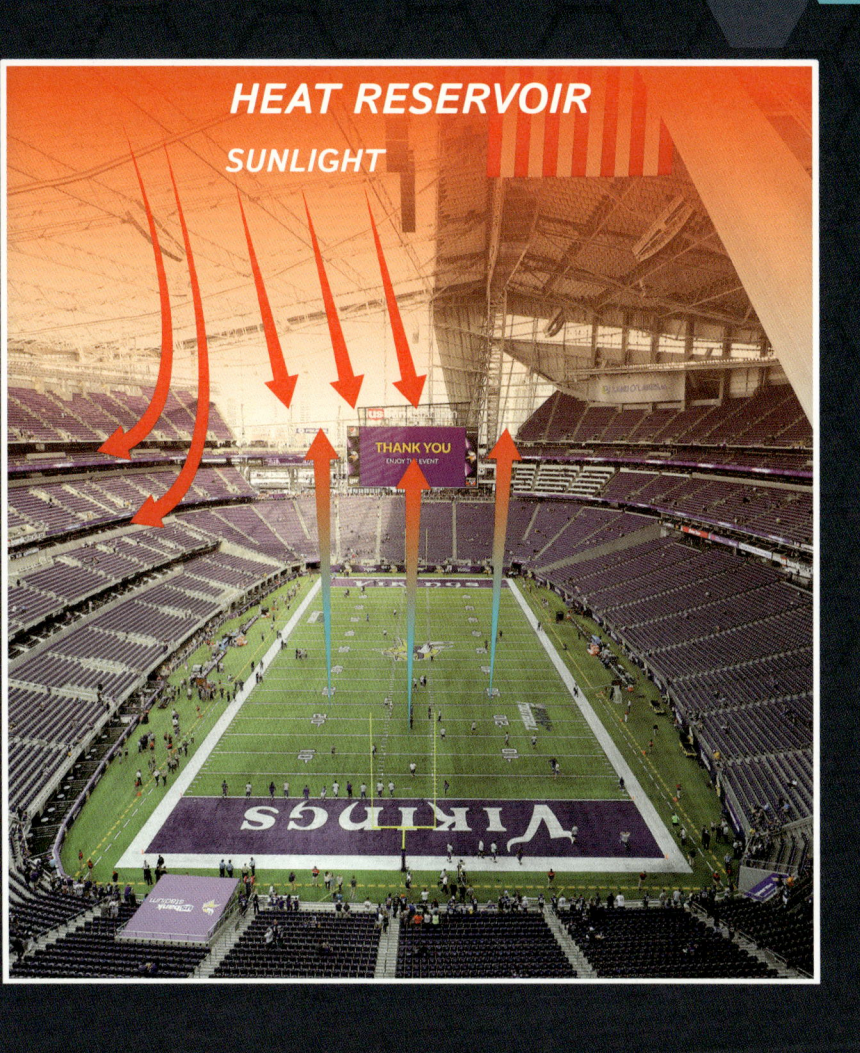

SUNLIGHT

U.S. Bank Stadium uses its south-facing clear roof to help heat the building on cold days. The sunlight shining through the roof warms the air near the roof, like a greenhouse. That warm air gets vented down into the stands. Warm air on the field rises up to the roof, where it can be vented back to the stands. The stadium still uses other heating methods, but it requires less energy to heat than the old, smaller stadium did.

HEATING A STADIUM

out on rollers. The stadium also includes a massive circular video screen overhead. The screen measures 58 feet (18 m) tall and 1,100 feet (335 m) around, the length of almost three football fields.

University of Phoenix Stadium (now State Farm Stadium) in Glendale, Arizona, hosted Super Bowl XLIX. This stadium has both a retractable roof and a retractable grass field. The 19-million-pound (8.6-million-kg) grass field is rolled in and out on steel rails. This allows the grass to grow outside in the sunshine between games.

STICKY GRIPS

Everything from indoor stadiums down to player equipment needs engineering. The engineering in equipment such as gloves can make a huge difference in performance. The improvements can be enough to change the sport of football. On January 21, 1979, in Super Bowl XIII, Dallas Cowboys tight end Jackie Smith raced to the end zone. Quarterback Roger Staubach

One of Mercedes-Benz Stadium's main features is its retractable roof.

threw him the ball. With no defenders near, the ball went directly to Smith. He brought both hands in and wrapped them around the ball. Unfortunately, the football escaped, bouncing off his chest and through his hands. The missed touchdown made all the difference. Smith and the Cowboys lost to the Pittsburgh Steelers 35–31. Compare this to Super Bowl XLII on February 3, 2008. With only 1:16 left in the game, New York Giants wide receiver David Tyree leaped high into the air to snag a ball. Even as he was pummeled by the defense, he gripped the ball with one hand and held it against his helmet. This amazing reception set the Giants up for their winning touchdown.

DIGGING IN FOR SPEED

Players cannot do their jobs if their feet slide on the turf. Athletic clothing maker Nike uses teams of designers, coaches, and athletes to develop specially made cleats for football shoes. These specialized shoes might include shovel, tri-star, or conical cleats. Each type grips the turf a special way depending on player movement.

Lester Hayes rubs Stickum on his hands during Super Bowl XV.

What was the difference between the two games? Sticky gloves. Sticky gloves were invented in the late 1990s. Before their invention, some players smeared a sticky mixture called Stickum on their hands and forearms. Oakland Raiders cornerback Lester Hayes

Silicone coats the palms and fingers of sticky gloves.

played in Super Bowl XV on January 25, 1981. Hayes was famous for covering his body with the substance. But Stickum was eventually banned. That didn't stop players from trying to find anything to help them grip the ball better. They tried glass cutter gloves and scuba diving gloves. They wanted something more.

That's when glove engineering stepped in. Sticky gloves are made of silicone. Silicone is a solid material with tacky properties. When it contacts a football, it microscopically acts like a sticky goop against the tiny bumps on the football. It's almost like trying to slide a football through honey-coated fingers. The gloves are stickier than a bare hand by approximately 20 percent. If Smith had worn a pair in 1979, it could have made all the difference.

Muhsin Muhammad catches the ball during Super Bowl XXXVIII.

CHAPTER **5**

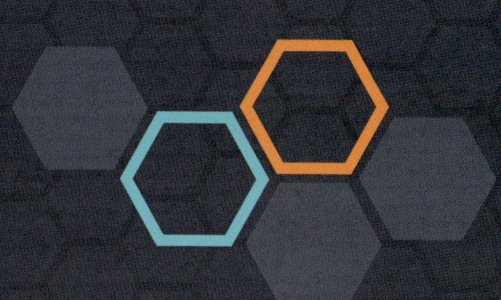

MATH IN ACTION

Algebra, geometry, and statistics are different types of math. Football uses each of them. Every play in the Super Bowl can be described with math. On February 1, 2004, in Super Bowl XXXVIII, Carolina Panthers quarterback Jake Delhomme connected on a pass to Muhsin Muhammad. The wide receiver caught the ball 51 yards downfield and ran another 34 yards for the touchdown. To make the play, the timing had to be perfect. Muhammad needed 9.8 seconds to run the 51 yards. Delhomme hurled

Algebra can describe how fast Delhomme needed to throw the football:

The equation is

$$\frac{d}{t} = r$$

or,

$$\frac{\text{distance (how far the football went)}}{\text{time (how many seconds)}} = \text{rate (speed of the football)}$$

The ball went 51 yards, so that is the number for "distance." It went that distance in 3.6 seconds, the number for "time." Dividing 51 by 3.6 gives the speed the football was traveling.

$$\frac{51 \text{ yards}}{3.6 \text{ seconds}} = \text{speed of the football} = \frac{14.2 \text{ yards}}{\text{second}}$$

That means the football was traveling 14.2 yards per second.

CALCULATING SPEED

the football the same distance in 3.6 seconds. To give Muhammad enough running time, Delhomme scrambled for 6.2 seconds before throwing the ball. This allowed the football to arrive in the wide receiver's hands exactly 51 yards downfield.

Algebra explains how fast the ball needs to travel to reach its destination. Delhomme threw the football at a speed of 14.2 yards per second to make the play. But that's not how the players think during a game. Using their years of experience, they automatically adjust their running speed or throwing power to make the play. In this case, the 85-yard touchdown remains the longest pass play in Super Bowl history through 2019.

ANGLING FOR THE WIN

Geometry is an area of math that deals with shapes and angles. It's important to the game of football. The offense and defense have two different objectives. The offense would like to run in a straight line directly toward the end zone to get as many yards as possible.

FLYING AND FOOTBALL

Members of the US Air Force Thunderbirds flying team sometimes do flyovers at Super Bowls. They have to time their arrival over the stadium so that it happens at exactly the right time. Pilots have to do math. They use information such as how far away the stadium is and how fast they are flying to get there at the right moment.

The defense would like to make the offensive players run sideways, not moving forward any yards. The more a defense can force the offense to run at an angle toward the sidelines, the fewer yards gained.

Another example of geometry in football can be seen in passes thrown by a quarterback. The quarterback has receivers running preselected routes. His job is to throw a pass to a point in space where the receiver and the football will intersect. He adjusts the power of his throw based on the angle and speed his receiver is running. Defenders do something similar. They use cutoff angles to tackle speedy runners.

In Super Bowl XLVII, Baltimore Ravens punter Sam Koch punted out of his own end zone. The ball came down near the San Francisco 45-yard line where Ted Ginn grabbed it. Ginn raced across the field and then down the opposite sideline toward the end zone. He might have scored, but Koch realized what was happening and angled toward the direction the speedy Ginn was running. He intersected with Ginn and knocked him out of bounds. Koch could not outrace Ginn, but using the proper angle, he could intercept him and make the tackle. Players may not be thinking about math, but they use it to their advantage.

STATISTICALLY SPEAKING

Every Super Bowl game is measured by statistics. They're announced during the game. They're printed in books. They're found all over the internet. No Super Bowl would be complete without them. In fact, the wide variety of statistics is amazing. Football fans might immediately think about player or team statistics. Two teams are tied at having lost the most Super Bowls. The Broncos and Patriots have lost five each. Tom Brady has the most passing yards in a Super Bowl. He threw for an incredible 505 yards in Super Bowl LII.

There are many more statistics. Super Bowl XIV, on January 20, 1980, had the highest attendance, with 103,985 fans in the stands of the Rose Bowl in Pasadena, California. It cost $5.25 million to air a 30-second television commercial during Super Bowl LIII. The future promises even more. More Super Bowls mean more statistics and more ways to find STEM integrated into this extraordinary game.

Sam Koch angles in for the tackle in Super Bowl XLVII.

GLOSSARY

concessions
Food, drinks, and other items sold at a game.

consecutive
In a row.

intercept
To stop something in the path it is moving on.

intersect
To meet at a certain point.

microscopically
Having to do with something so small it can't be seen without a microscope.

preselected
Chosen or planned in advance.

pylon
A tower or pillar, such as the orange posts at the corners of the end zones.

retractable roof
A roof that can open and close.

roster
A list of players on a team.

synchronized
Set to happen at the same time.

MORE INFORMATION

BOOKS

Abdo, Kenny. *Super Bowl*. Minneapolis, MN: Abdo Publishing, 2019.

Martin, Brett S. *STEM in Football*. Minneapolis, MN: Abdo Publishing, 2018.

Wilner, Barry. *Ultimate NFL Road Trip*. Minneapolis, MN: Abdo Publishing, 2019.

ONLINE RESOURCES

Booklinks
NONFICTION NETWORK
FREE! ONLINE NONFICTION RESOURCES

To learn more about STEM in the Super Bowl, visit **abdobooklinks.com** or scan this QR code. These links are routinely monitored and updated to provide the most current information available.

INDEX

Air Force Thunderbirds, US, 42
Atlanta Falcons, 23

Baltimore Ravens, 43

Carolina Panthers, 39
CBS, 25–26
Chicago Bears, 15–17

Dallas Cowboys, 32–34
Delhomme, Jake, 39–41
Denver Broncos, 25, 44
Dyson, Kevin, 6–7

Elway, John, 25

Ginn, Ted, 43
Green Bay Packers, 18
Grossman, Rex, 15

Hayes, Lester, 35–37

Indianapolis Colts, 15–17

Jones, Mike, 6–7

Kansas City Chiefs, 18
Kay, Clarence, 25
Koch, Sam, 43

Manning, Peyton, 17
McNair, Steve, 6
Minnesota Vikings, 8
Muhammad, Muhsin, 39–41

NBC, 26
New England Patriots, 11, 23, 44
New York Giants, 11, 25, 34
Nike, 34

Oakland Raiders, 35

Philadelphia Eagles, 11
Pittsburgh Steelers, 11, 34

Reid, Gabe, 17
Rose Bowl, 44

Seattle Seahawks, 8
Skycam, 21, 22, 26
Smith, Jackie, 32–34, 37
St. Louis Rams, 5–7
Stickum, 35–37

Taylor, Lawrence, 15
Tennessee Titans, 5–6
Tyree, David, 34

White, James, 23

ABOUT THE AUTHOR

Mike Downs is an author, a pilot, and the father of three great kids. He loves writing, going on adventures, and teaching kids new and exciting things. He also enjoys watching the Super Bowl.

3 1524 00744 0623